108

beads

poems on the way

jason b. fischer

iUniverse, Inc.
New York   Bloomington

108 Beads
poems on the way

iUniverse books may be ordered through booksellers or by contacting:

iUniverse
1663 Liberty Drive
Bloomington, IN 47403
www.iuniverse.com
1-800-Authors (1-800-288-4677)

ISBN: 978-1-4401-1558-5 (sc)
ISBN: 978-1-4401-1559-2 (ebk)

Printed in the United States of America

iUniverse rev. date: 7/7/2009

To Bong Dal Kim,
modern ancient, teacher and friend.

introduction

Here are 108 poems written by a man more than a decade my junior. I owe him much for the person I have become to this day, having almost shamelessly capitalized on his many years of inquiry and practice. I admire him, the fearlessness and abandon with which he dedicated his life so completely to self-cultivation, exploration, and growth. He was a true aspirant, traveling with eyes and heart opened in a way I wonder if I myself could ever hope to duplicate.

Inspired by Buddhist and Taoist teachings and tales of homeless, wandering poets like Han Shan, Basho, and Ryokan, he left behind family and friends seeking to learn more and live more. His was a path that, over four years time, coursed through India and Thailand, Korea, China and Tibet, as well as centers of Buddhist learning in the States, a path that culminated in his ordaining as a Theravadin Buddhist monk, and then disrobing. His few belongings throughout consisted of rarely more than a single change of clothes, an oversized journal, and a handful of pens with which to note his thoughts and experiences, in poems, on the way.

The onus is on me to speak for that person now, a challenge I approach with caution and humility. After all, it is my idea to publish his writings, not his. For this, I may owe him an apology, one I will gladly tender should he ever request this of me. I would welcome the conversation.

Austin, Texas
2009

beads

1 •

They may accuse me of wasting my life

They may accuse me of wasting my life,
but what can I do?
There are no certain terms to explain these things.
An hour's standing in a smiling storm.
The bend of a leafless tree.
A single noon with pavilion birds.
A circle. A square. A sphere.
Nothing suffices, but that still
I should continue sure in my knowing
that nothing remains
better than most things.

2.

They tell me I am unreasonable

They tell me I am unreasonable
to want to do nothing.
How will you pay, they ask.
I will pay with my heart.

3.

I lead a worthless life

I lead a worthless life,
writing a few poems now and then.
What am I accomplishing by it?
Nothing special.

4•

A river dies

A river dies
if you try to make it straight.
In such a way I cannot be channeled
to irrigate the crops and fields.
I must course through valleys,
roll past towns and amble
toward the infinite ocean.
Nature has made me useless.

5.

I would rather live fully

I would rather live fully
for just one moment
than partially for a millennium.
And if I should someday slip
from the cliff's edge because of this,
let it be known
I want not to be mended.
I will have lived already.

6.

A plant bends toward light

A plant bends toward light
without volition.
My gravitations are the same way.
Do not ask me why I live as I do.
How should I know why?

7.

I cannot apologize

I cannot apologize
for anything I do.
I am like a fire that consumes a house.
Who can blame the fire?
I only follow my heart.

8.

The moon and sun

The moon and sun
both roam without wallets
and I have never seen a cloud
carry a purse.
Drifting along like this,
how can I differ?
I approach the Buddha
only with nothing to offer.

9·

Zen Master Dogen cautioned

Zen Master Dogen cautioned,
"Do not look at big fish."
But for me this entire realm
is a big fish,
so how should I stop looking?

10 •

Do me a favor

Do me a favor
and do not call me a Buddhist.
My heart is my Buddhism.

11 •

My monastery walls

My monastery walls
are daily twice painted red.
And the temple bell here
which calls me to service
rings incessantly.
I am no monk.
And I am no poet.

12 •

Take out my tongue

Take out my tongue.
Make it into a belt or purse,
fold it into a child's toy,
or use it as a doorstop.
I care not.
For if the useless in this world
must find its use,
then I release it freely knowing
that I will cry and laugh and love
forever all the same.

13.

Unable to write, I write

Unable to write, I write.
Why not?
Even the weed
casts an exact shadow.

14 •

Why would the lotus ever leave

Why would the lotus ever leave
its home within the mud?
Eventually it has to.

15 •

To others it seems that I

To others it seems that I
have shirked all responsibility.
No paycheck. No home.
I undertake a different task.
What greater obligation have I
than this?

16•

I journey only

I journey only
so I may better
be still.

17·

I live this life

I live this life
feeding my heart,
a desert nomad
tending his only goat.

18•

Thieves cannot steal

Thieves cannot steal
from other thieves or from those
who have nothing.
I have only that
which has me.
Perhaps someday I will have nothing.
Until then, this.

19.

I am a farmer

I am a farmer
unable to ensure a good crop.
The elements master me,
and not the other way around.
I turn the soil, seed it and wait.
If one pumpkin surfaces,
it's one pumpkin more than before.

20•

I long for the quiet place

I long for the quiet place.
"The quiet place is your heart."
Then I long for my heart.

21 •

In Thailand

A schoolyard of children,
three, maybe four hundred
allow me to play god and table tennis with them.
They think I look like Buddha.
I cannot help but smile
in embarrassment and gratitude
at even the one who, smiling himself,
gives me the finger.

22 •

In school they taught me well

In school they taught me well
how to treat my mind like a mule,
pack my things upon it
and goad it up the slope.
Yet why should I?
If it wants to ascend, I let it.
If it wants to descend, I let it.
If it wants to remain, I let it.
High and low, up and down,
my mule and I
travel as companions.

23.

Water cannot rest on a slope

Water cannot rest on a slope
and rain will not hide
forever in a cloud.
Even a seed
which adores the earth
must sprout.

24.

Take not from me my sorrow

Take not from me my sorrow
for without it I might wonder
if I were real.

25 •

My heart is big despite

My heart is big despite
a use for smallness,
nested awkward in my chest like a mountain
in a niche meant for a stone.
Whether I suffer or mind because of this
is not such an important matter.

26·

No boat owns the ocean

No boat owns the ocean
and a boat with no rudder
goes where the ocean goes.
At my helm there is no one.
Joy and sorrow?
Neither are mine to captain.

27.

I smile

I smile
not because I do not suffer,
but because I do.

28.

Wisdom is an eel

Wisdom is an eel
and none of my hands have fingers.
The inner voice counsels,
"Let your fingerlessness enlighten."

29.

I wander and I roam

I wander and I roam
alone yet never alone
carrying with me this
the one and precious note
I cannot name.
It hums along in my heart.

30 •

Luckily I am reminded

Luckily I am reminded
reading Rumi, Hafiz, Frost, T'ao Ch'ien,
that I am really quite a lousy poet
and then am quickly freed
to continue.

31 •

Walking and walking I beg of my heart

Walking and walking I beg of my heart,
show me a destination for my wander.
"But you are already here."
So walking along I tell it again:
Yes I know, heart.
Already I know.

32.

All this talk of destinies

All this talk of destinies,
I don't know a thing about it.
My vision?
I am a blind frog in a bog.
I am fungus on the tree root.
I am a castaway leaf
dispersed by the innocent breeze.

33.

Sometimes I catch myself longing

Sometimes I catch myself longing
for it all to be less simple.
There is comfort in struggle
and a discomfort in ease.
I ask for harder riddles,
beseeching the obvious
become obfuscated.
It never works.

34.

The True Masters

The True Masters
are so ordinary,
nothing special about them at all.

35·

All day I excavate

All day I excavate
a hole for my sadness.
Yet when night descends
and the red moon rises,
laughter overtakes my heart.
I frolic in such a good joke.
Me the one in charge?
Hysterical!

36·

Water that comes from the spring

Water that comes from the spring
does not belong to the spring.
I am an ignorant man.

37.

Why try to be perfect

Why try to be perfect,
when you can perfectly be?

38.

Do not try to tell me

Do not try to tell me
that self does not exist.
Self exists but distinction does not.
Self as separate from other?
Now there's the real illusion.

39.

Enlightenment is a dewdrop

Enlightenment is a dewdrop
too cleverly disguised
as a diamond.

40•

Life is suffering

Life is suffering.
Or maybe it's not.

41.

The very best Buddhist

The very best Buddhist
is not a Buddhist at all.
The master no longer
dwells in a small hut.

42·

Religions may differ

Religions may differ,
but masters cannot.
When any two meet to debate,
they smile and nod in agreement.

43·

All opposites are crest and trough

All opposites are crest and trough
of one wave perpetually folding
back and then forth.
Even Enlightenment
migrates toward confusion.
How can there be any exceptions?

44.

Enlightenment is nothing

Enlightenment is nothing
but the joyful embrace
of bafflement.

45.

My heart always knows

My heart always knows
what I do not know,
for it is a piece of the universe.

46•

Coal need not

Coal need not
be cut into diamond
to shine.

47.

I am

I am
perfect,
flawed.

48.

If mining for treasure, stop right there

If mining for treasure, stop right there.
Drop the pickax.
Wipe your brow.
Breathe deep the scent of the cave.

49 •

Those who hoard misunderstand

Those who hoard misunderstand.
Why keep for one's self anything
that is not worth sharing?

50 •

The greatest gratitude I can have

The greatest gratitude I can have
is for my birth.
With this
even when I suffer
I suffer with appreciation.

51•

I am without eyes

I am without eyes.
The whole of it all
passionate wild profound
is itself vision
enough for me.

52 •

There are no dull situations

There are no dull situations,
no dull persons, no dull lives.
Be alert
and the whole world fascinates.

53·

The path discovered

The path discovered
is the path accomplished.
Nothing left to try for,
the pilgrimage is Mecca.

54.

You are

You are.
You do not become.

55 •

Attacking is tiring

Attacking is tiring.
Defending is tiring.
Those who truly want peace
decline all invitations
to battle.

56·

Do not emulate the Buddha

Do not emulate the Buddha.
He is unworthy.
To be more like the Enlightened,
be more like you.

57.

Being is knowing

Being is knowing
and not the other
way around.

58.

Ten thousand miles now

Ten thousand miles now
from the place of my birth
with each breath I'm reminded
of where I am always
home.

59•

To Gil

Discussing Enlightenment
on a bamboo bed in the jungle,
we agree and disagree.
The cobra that passes us has
the final word on the matter.
We watch in admiration and smile.

60.

If the Buddha is

If the Buddha is
within the temple,
what is without?

61•

My things balled in a corner

My things balled in a corner,
worn sandals by the door,
these days I make my wanderings
sitting still.
First down to the ocean,
then up to the mountain's peak.
Back and forth I go
nowhere.

62 •

Holding nothing I am

Holding nothing I am
held completely.
Empty-handedness
enables the embrace.

63.

The Noble Two-Fold Path

The Noble Two-Fold Path:
Learn how to meditate.
Forget how to meditate.
The rest takes care of itself.

64 •

Meditation is the challenge

Meditation is the challenge
of having to summit a mountain
whose peak can be found
only upon the ground.

65.

My meditation practice grows

My meditation practice grows
duller and duller.
The more ordinary it becomes,
the more extraordinary it becomes.
The more extraordinary it becomes,
the more ordinary I discover
it has been all along.

66 •

Life is hard. Practice is hard

Life is hard. Practice is hard.
Without practice, there can be no relief.
With practice, there can be no relief either.
But there can be...

67.

Do not step outside

Do not step outside
when there is no outside to step into.
Don't watch your breathing
with your mind.
In meditation, everything breathes.
Mind, breath, body.
Where is there any separation?

68.

Do not meditate

Do not meditate.
You are ore for the forge,
dough for the oven,
clay for the kiln.
The work is not yours.
Let meditation meditate.

69.

People ask me how to meditate

People ask me how to meditate
but it is too easy to research on one's own.
Just sit there,
with no thought of gain.

70 •

Seek whatever you must

Seek whatever you must
to first find the cushion,
then cease seeking altogether.
It will have served its only purpose.

71 •

Thinking is other than thought, distinguish

Thinking is other than thought, distinguish.
Thinking forces. Thought allows.
The sail that pulls the boat
does so not when flapping.

72.

All sorts of creatures

All sorts of creatures
crawl on us during meditation.
Once a cat climbed onto my head.
"What's that?" I thought.
But still I did not move.

73.

Meditation

A thousand leaves on the tree
each wind passing through sounds like
yesterday a purple flower

74 •

From an unknowing of unknowing

From an unknowing of unknowing,
a knowing of unknowing,
a knowing of knowing,
an unknowing of knowing.

75•

The opera plays

The opera plays
into an empty apartment.
Is this all?

76.

On Er Mei Mountain

Perfectly undisturbed.
Snow on the high winter branches.
Death. Life.

77.

If I were forced to choose

If I were forced to choose
just two words to use
for the rest of my days,
I would need only these:
thank you.

78.

To be content even

To be content even
with our discontent
is to solve the riddle.

79·

A monk now

A monk now,
what difference does it make?
Thankfully,
none at all.

80 •

Having at last traded

Having at last traded
all my wine in for water,
I remain drunk nonetheless.
Traipsing about in a single cloth,
nothing makes me sober.

81 •

Walking on almsround

Walking on almsround,
a small taste of the old way.
The dawning sun places
just a few grains
into an empty bowl.

82.

The moon, half-drunk half-sober

The moon, half-drunk half-sober,
still has not left by dawn.
A long night with a good friend.
I walk it to the morning gate
then sweep the temple grounds,
free of petals and leaves.

83.

I am a beggar

I am a beggar
entering meditation like
a monk enters towns.
Doors open
and I must accept
all that falls in my bowl.

84 •

The smart are smart but

The smart are smart but
they envy the wise.
And because they envy the wise
they try to make themselves
smarter and smarter.
This is like running westward
to catch a glimpse of dawn.

85.

Each morning we sweep

Each morning we sweep
not to clear a path,
but because
each morning we sweep.

86 •

To Kitisampano

Game after game laughing
two monks neglect their practice.
I seemed to have forgotten something,
but I cannot remember what.
Ah, this is the thing!

87.

When the monks' chants cease

When the monks' chants cease
only then do the sutras emerge.
Morning birds in every tree
echo the endless teachings.

88.

To Kitisampano

By your leaving I'm reminded
of the thousand times I've left a thousand friends
gleefully to wander on my own.
But not today.
Today I am the staying one.
Is this what I have done to others?
How cruel of me.

89.

The more I seek solitude

The more I seek solitude,
the more I encounter friendship.
I do not find what I seek.
What I seek finds me.

90 •

To Kitisampano

I want to write a poem
about your departure
but the only words I have
sit like stones:
I am sad you're leaving.

91 •

I am a solitary man

I am a solitary man
who savors populated streets.
And I am a social man
who chooses a windowless house.
In my pocket there's a folded message
an invitation
sent from the sun, grasses and flies.
Come & play, it says.
Come & play.

92.

If the Buddha is like a lotus

If the Buddha is like a lotus,
then perhaps I am more like the carp.
If for lifetimes I am to swim
amidst the murk and muck,
then who am I to argue?
This will be fine too.

93•

Rain that falls on one mountain

Rain that falls on one mountain
cannot roll down
the slopes of another.

94.

Learned of my leaving

Learned of my leaving,
Monk Gumon consoled best,
"Maybe in the next life
you will be born a Buddhist."

95•

I entered the temple

I entered the temple
to sever my ties with the world,
but only fell deeper in love.
What's a fool like this to do?
I fold my robe, upturn my bowl,
and walk
bare into the break of waves.

96 ○

ceremony

ceremony abbot chants i kneel draped in orange palms together head shaven and bowed mind reeling and doubt what am i doing leaving this life? uncertainties swarming like hornets what am i doing leaving? the temple a hive my brother monks buzzing pali watching on such heat and frenzy i sweat tear up resist these final moments what am i doing? the abbot reaching grabs holds the robe belt knot seconds dwindling is this a mistake? time expiring vanished to shout Stop! pulled shuddered off balance jarred toppling and that's it the sash loosed from trunk captured lifeless in grasp the great cloth collapsed slipped fallen from shoulder a molted skin in heap piled what have i done? exposed unhidden perspiring thick febrile burning searing broiling shame grief what have i done? what have i done? the answer arriven sudden a breeze soothing cooling as if unseen resting a hand on skin calming countless pores thirsting awakened hearing knowing listening to the now here Buddha silent graceful formless vast leaned in to whisper secret reply ancient hushed the missive response voiced unvoiced to atoms cells muscle bone hair flesh *What are you doing?* no thought *Isn't it obvious?* no mind *You are entering* just this? *You are entering*

97•

My head no longer shaven

My head no longer shaven
I keep it shaggily as
a sign of my attachment.
After all,
I am attached,
as sure as I am human.

98.

Befriend

Befriend,
starting first with yourself.
Befriend.

99·

Those who transcend

Those who transcend
cry when crying,
laugh when laughing,
yawn when yawning.

100 •

Do unto others

Do unto others
as you would have them
do unto others.

101 •

Lights off, the incense burns

Lights off, the incense burns.
Just sitting let me push off sleep
to remain a while longer please
awake and free of dream.

102 •

To love is to live life well

To love is to live life well.
And to be loved in return,
absolutely irrelevant.

103 •

If you must remember something

If you must remember something,
remember to forget,
so you may live each moment anew.

104 •

The poem I have spent my life writing

The poem I have spent my life writing
would not be worth reading.
After all, to others
it would not look like much.
Just a list of the names
of those I have loved.
Though to me such a poem
would say it all.

105•

Ignore the masters

Ignore the masters.
Ignore the great texts.
Eat the True Path.

106•

I am not my fault

I am not my fault.
You are not yours.
We suffer and fail sometimes.
And that's the whole story.

107•

I have nothing to say

I have nothing to say.
No more so than an ant
or a swamp-reed
or a stone.
Those who take meaning from my poems
are like those who pass a pond in daylight
and spy the moon.

108•

Never mind

Never mind.